Parents and Caregivers,

Stone Arch Readers are designed to provide enjoyable reading experiences, as well as opportunities to develop vocabulary, literacy skills, and comprehension. Here are a few ways to support your beginning reader:

- Talk with your child about the ideas addressed in the story.

- Discuss each illustration, mentioning the characters, where they are, and what they are doing.

- Read with expression, pointing to each word. You may want to read the whole story through and then revisit parts of the story to ensure that the meanings of words or phrases are understood.

- Talk about why the character did what he or she did and what your child would do in that situation.

- Help your child connect with characters and events in the story.

Remember, reading with your child should be fun, not forced. Each moment spent reading with your child is a priceless investment in his or her literacy life.

Gail Saunders-Smith, Ph.D.

STONE ARCH READERS

are published by Stone Arch Books, a Capstone Imprint
1710 Roe Crest Drive
North Mankato, Minnesota 56003
www.capstonepub.com

Library of Congress Cataloging-in-Publication Data
Klein, Adria F. (Adria Fay), 1947-
Big Train takes a trip / by Adria Klein ; illustrated by Craig Cameron.
p. cm. -- (Stone Arch readers: Train time)
Summary: Big Train makes sure that all his cars are lined up before starting a trip.
ISBN 978-1-4342-4781-0 (library binding) -- ISBN 978-1-4342-6194-6 (pbk.)
1. Locomotives--Juvenile fiction. 2. Railroad trains--Juvenile fiction.
[1. Locomotives--Fiction. 2. Railroad trains--Fiction.] I. Cameron, Craig, ill. II. Title.
PZ7.K678324Bim 2013
[E]--dc23   2012046899

Reading Consultants:
Gail Saunders-Smith, Ph.D.
Melinda Melton Crow, M.Ed.
Laurie K. Holland, Media Specialist
Designer: Russell Griesmer

Printed in China by Nordica.
0413/CA21300422
032013   007226NORDF13

Big Train
Takes a Trip

written by
Adria F. Klein

illustrated by
Craig Cameron

STONE ARCH BOOKS
a capstone imprint

Engine and his friends
were taking a trip.

"It is time to go,"
said Engine.

"We are ready," the train
cars said.

"I will be first in line,"
Engine said. "Who will
go next?"

"I will," the green car said.

"Get in line," Engine said.

"Who will go next?"
Engine said.

"I will," the blue car said.

"Get in line," Engine said.

"Who will go last?"
Engine said.

"I will," the brown car said.

"Get in line," Engine said.

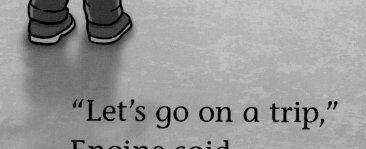

"Let's go on a trip,"
Engine said.

Toot! Toot!

STORY WORDS

engine   green   brown

friends   blue

Word Count: 88

STONE ARCH READERS

Circus Train and the Clowns

written by
Adria F. Klein
Illustrated by
Craig Cameron

STONE ARCH READERS

City Train in Trouble

written by
Adria F. Klein
Illustrated by
Craig Cameron

STONE ARCH READERS

The Full Freight Train

written by
Adria F. Klein
Illustrated by
Craig Cameron